A 20th C...

A Don Bluth/Gary Goldman Film

Adapted by Kari James
Illustrated by Josie Yee

🏵 A GOLDEN BOOK • NEW YORK

Golden Books Publishing Company, Inc., New York, New York 10106

™ & © 1997 Twentieth Century Fox Film Corporation. All rights reserved. Printed in the U.S.A. No part of this book may be reproduced or copied in any form without written permission from the copyright owner. GOLDEN BOOKS®, A GOLDEN BOOK®, A LITTLE GOLDEN BOOK®, G DESIGN™, and the distinctive gold spine are trademarks of Golden Books Publishing Company, Inc. Library of Congress Catalog Card Number: 97-70004   ISBN: 0-307-98805-8   First Edition 1997
A MCMXCVII

Once upon a time, back in the glittering days of Imperial Russia, the empress Marie gave a special gift to her beloved granddaughter, Anastasia Romanov. It was a beautiful music box.

Marie wound up the box with a pretty little flower-shaped key on a gold necklace.

"It plays our lullaby!" cried Anastasia.

"After I go home to Paris, you can play it before you go to sleep, and pretend that it's me singing," said Marie. "This key says 'Together in Paris.' Soon you and I will be, my darling."

But that evening, as they enjoyed themselves at a grand ball in the Imperial Palace, Marie and Anastasia could not know that their lives were about to change forever.

Suddenly the music stopped. Dancing couples halted. The ballroom echoed with the loud footsteps of a tall, evil-looking man named Rasputin.

People stepped back from this man as he stalked toward Anastasia's father, Czar Nicholas of Russia.

"Rasputin! How dare you return to the palace!" cried Nicholas.

"You cannot banish the great Rasputin," the evil man retorted. "Mark my words. You and the entire Romanov family will die within the fortnight!"

Rasputin raised a large reliquary over his head. It shot a bolt of lightning to the chandelier above, which fell with a crash. People screamed in the sudden darkness. When the light was finally restored, Rasputin had disappeared.

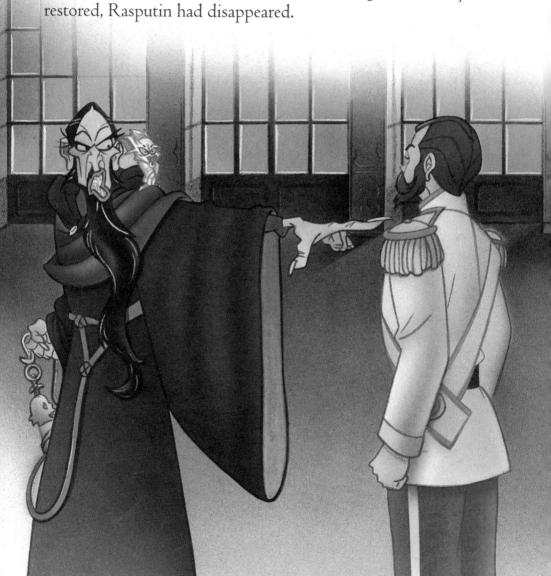

Before he had been banished from the palace, Rasputin had been considered almost a member of the royal family. Now, he had sold his soul to the devil in order to destroy the Romanovs. He used his dark powers to persuade a mob of unhappy Russians to storm the Winter Palace and attack the czar and his family.

No one saw the royal family again after that night, but a small servant boy named Dimitri helped Anastasia and Marie escape with their lives. And it was Dimitri who found the music box that they left behind in their haste.

Many hundreds of people tried to get on the train out of
Russia that terrible night. Marie and Anastasia were among
them. Some people pulled Marie on board.

"Anastasia! Take my hand!" shouted Marie.

"Grandmama!" cried Anastasia. She was bumped and pushed by the panicky crowd as everyone tried to get on the train, and her small hand slipped from Marie's grasp. Anastasia tripped and fell to the ground as the train whistle blew.

"Anastasia!" screamed Marie. But she could do nothing as the train pulled away, leaving the little girl unconscious on the ground.

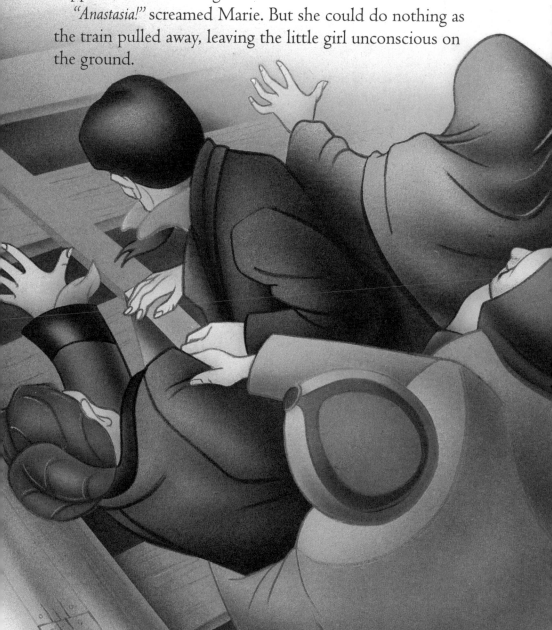

Somehow, life in Russia went on after that horrible day. Anastasia grew up in an orphanage, where she was given the name Anya, as she could not remember anything about her past. But she held tightly to the key that said "Together in Paris," and wondered if her real life awaited her there.

Ten years later, Anya and her dog, Pooka, set off for the old palace. There, she had heard, she could find a young man named Dimitri, who could help her get traveling papers for Paris.

Dimitri was indeed inside the palace, making plans with his friend Vladimir.

"It's all set," said Dimitri. "We'll find a girl to play the part of Anastasia. We'll teach her what to say. Then it's off to Paris. When Empress Marie sees this music box, she'll think we've brought the real Anastasia. She'll pay us all that reward money that everyone's been talking about. We'll be rich!"

Just then, Dimitri and Vladimir heard a noise. It was Anya and Pooka exploring the palace.

"Vlad, do you see what I see?" whispered Dimitri excitedly.

This strange young girl looked just like the young Anastasia in the portrait on the wall! The men knew they had found the perfect girl for their scheme.

"Are you Dimitri?" asked Anya. "Can you help me get to Paris?"

"Oddly enough, we're going to Paris ourselves," said Dimitri. He looked closely at Anya. "Did it ever occur to you that you resemble the grand duchess Anastasia?" he asked her.

It didn't take long for Dimitri and Vladimir to convince Anya to go with them to visit the empress once they got to Paris.

"After all," said Anya, "if I don't remember who I am, then who's to say I'm not a grand duchess?"

It was at this time that Bartok, Rasputin's bat, traveled to the netherworld to find his master, who was trapped there, neither dead nor alive. Bartok wanted to inform Rasputin that he hadn't succeeded in destroying all the Romanovs, and that Anastasia, now called Anya, was still alive.

"Little Anya, beware!" screamed Rasputin. "In the dark of the night, evil will find you. Then my curse will be complete!"

Rasputin sent his minions to wreck the train that carried Anya and her companions. But, just as before, he was not powerful enough to destroy her.

Anya and her fellow travelers made it safely to the ship that would take them to Paris. Once on board, Dimitri bought Anya a dress.

"Marvelous!" exclaimed Vladimir. "Anya, now that you're dressed for a ball, you will learn how to dance at one!"

So, Anya and Dimitri began to practice a waltz. They found it surprisingly easy to dance with each other.

"You look beautiful in that dress," Dimitri whispered.

Finally the travelers arrived in the magnificent city of Paris. It was Dimitri's last chance to make sure Anya remembered everything he had told her about the Romanovs.

"Empress Marie will ask you lots of questions," he warned her.

But it turned out that the empress was no longer receiving girls who were claiming to be Anastasia. She had given up hope of ever finding her beloved granddaughter.

Dimitri had slowly come to realize that Anya was not just a girl pretending to be Grand Duchess Anastasia—she *was* Anastasia. Dimitri also realized that he was falling in love with her, and it was sad to think that soon she would live in a world much different from his own.

But one night, for Anya's sake, he disguised himself as Marie's chauffeur and delivered the music box to the old woman. He knew that the empress would agree to meet Anya once she had seen the box—and he was right.

When Empress Marie came to visit Anya, she saw the key that the young woman was wearing around her neck. "May I?" she asked, reaching for it.

Then Marie took the music box from her evening bag. And, as the music began to play, Anya began to remember.

"The music box . . ." she murmured. ". . . To sing me to sleep when you were back in Paris . . . Oh, Grandmama, I remember!"

"You *are* Anastasia!" cried Marie. "My Anastasia, at last!"

The night grew later and later as Anastasia and her grandmother shared their family memories.

"Anastasia," said Marie, "in your laughter, once again I hear my Nicky, my son, your dear father. And you have also the beauty of your mother, Princess Alexandra, empress of all Russia."

The next morning, Marie sent for Dimitri.

"Here you are, Dimitri," said Marie, "ten million rubles, as promised, with my gratitude."

"I accept your gratitude, Your Highness," Dimitri said. "But I don't want the money."

"You were the boy, weren't you—the servant boy who got us out? You saved Anastasia's life, and mine," said Marie, "yet you want no reward?"

"I must go," Dimitri replied. He bowed and left quickly, for he knew that all the money in the world could not take the place of his Anastasia. There was nothing left for him to do now but go home to St. Petersburg.

Soon after, Empress Marie held a ball in honor of her granddaughter.

"Look at the people dance!" exclaimed Marie. "Like me, they are thrilled to welcome you to Paris."

"I know," said Anastasia. "It makes me so . . . happy." But secretly, she missed Dimitri.

Marie knew what Anastasia was thinking. "He didn't take the money, my dear," she said with a sigh. "There is no place for Dimitri beside the grand duchess Anastasia. But whatever life you may choose, I will hold you in my heart always."

The time had come for Anastasia to make a choice between her new life as a grand duchess or a life with Dimitri.

Meanwhile, Dimitri had decided to stay in Paris and tell
Anastasia that he loved her.

He walked by the palace gardens just as Anastasia was
leaving the ball—and just in time to help her fight Rasputin,
who had come to find the girl and destroy her once and
for all.

But when Rasputin harmed Dimitri, it was Anastasia who grabbed the evil man's reliquary and smashed it to bits. Without the reliquary, Rasputin was powerless. His body turned into a skeleton and then crumbled into dust.

Anastasia never regretted leaving the glittering life of royalty behind her. Her journey to her past was finally over. She had found her family, a home, and love—at last!